If Animals Kissed Good Night

Ann Whitford Paul

Pictures by David Walker

Farrar Straus Giroux
New York

For the most kissable Hazel Jane —A.W.P.

For Ben and Ellie —D.W.

Farrar Straus Giroux Books for Young Readers
An imprint of Macmillan Publishing Group, LLC
120 Broadway, New York, NY 10271

Color separations by Chroma Graphics PTE Ltd.
Printed in China by RR Donnelley Asia Printing Solutions Ltd., Dongguan City, Guangdong Province
First edition, 2008
First board book edition, 2014
All About Books paperback ISBN 978-1-4668-9989-6
3   5   7   9   10   8   6   4

mackids.com

Board book ISBN 978-0-374-30021-0

Library of Congress Cataloging-in-Publication Data
Paul, Ann Whitford.
    If animals kissed good night / Ann Whitford Paul ; pictures by David Walker.— 1st ed.
        p.   cm.
    Summary: Rhyming text explores what would happen if animals kissed like humans do, from a slow kiss
between a sloth and her cub to a mud-happy kiss from a hippo calf to his father.
    ISBN 978-0-374-38051-9
    [1. Kissing—Fiction.   2. Animals—Habits and behavior—Fiction.   3. Parent and child—Fiction.
4. Stories in rhyme.]   I. Walker, David, ill.   II. Title.

PZ7.P278338 If 2008
[E]—dc22
                                                                                                          2006051108

Farrar Straus Giroux Books for Young Readers may be purchased for business or promotional use.
For information on bulk purchases please contact Macmillan Corporate and Premium Sales Department
at (800) 221-7945 x5442 or by email at specialmarkets@macmillan.com.

If animals kissed
like we kiss good night,

Sloth
and her cub
in late afternoon's light
would hang from a tree
and start kissing

soooo slooowwwww . . .

the sky would turn pink
and the sun sink down low.

Peacock and chick

would spin a fan dance
and kiss with a kickity
high-stepping prance.

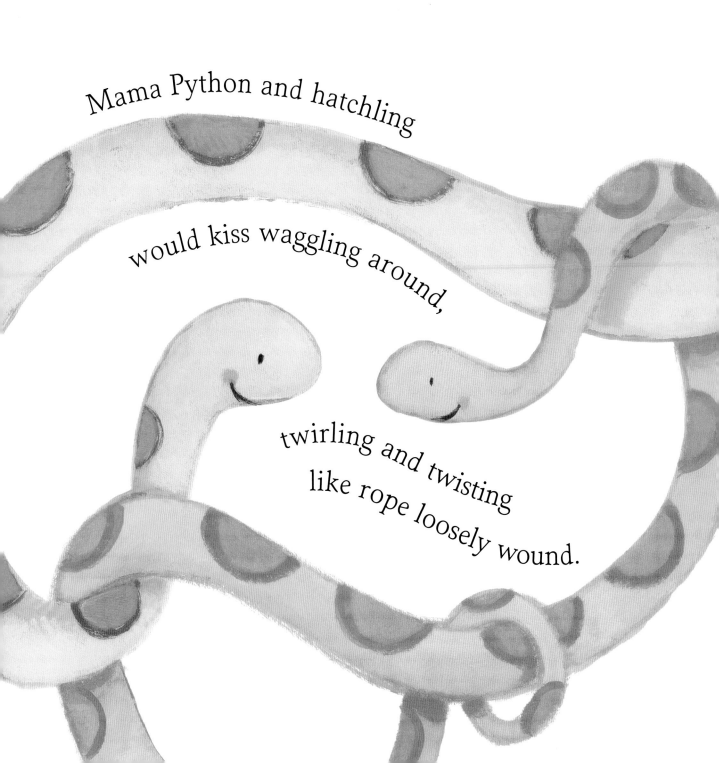

Mama Python and hatchling

would kiss waggling around,

twirling and twisting
like rope loosely wound.

Walrus calf and her papa
would make whiskery swishes,
rubbing each other
in scritch-scratchy kisses.

Mama Elephant's trunk would kiss and then sway

and shower her calf with a wet, washing spray.

If animals kissed like we kiss good night,
the sky would turn dull, the moon a chalk white—
and Sloth and her cub?

Still . . . kissing good night.

Parrot and chick
would klick-klack their beaks,
kissing klick-a-klack,
klick-a-klack,
klick-a-klack,
kleek.

Wolf and his pup
would kiss and then

HOWL!

Bear and her cub
would kiss
and then
GROWL!

Mama Monkey
and infant would
SWIII–IIING
through the trees,
smacking their lips
in a kissing trapeze.

Seal and his calf would blow big bubbled kisses

that rise to the surface
in splashity splishes.

If animals kissed like we kiss good night,
the sky would turn dark with the moon glowing white—
and Sloth and her cub?

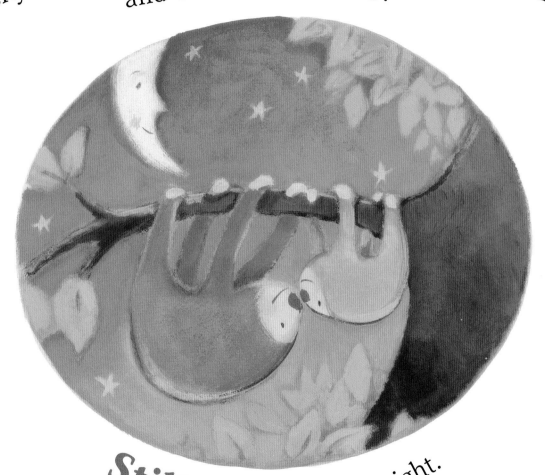

Still . . . kissing good night.

Mama Penguin and chick would stumble and slide

on slippery rocks in a hug-and-kiss ride.

Papa Rhino and calf
would kiss tip-a-tap-tap—
smooching their horns
in a **tip-a-tap rap.**

Giraffe
and his calf
would stretch
their necks
high
and kiss
just beneath
the top
of the sky.

Kangaroo and her joey
would jumpity-jump,
kiss, kiss, kiss, kiss,
bounce bumpity-bump.

Hippo calf would kiss Papa,
then they'd settle

down deep

in the slithery ooze—
a mud-happy heap.

If animals kissed
like we kiss good night,

the sky would turn black,

the moon would shine bright,

all would grow quiet
with all tucked in tight—

but Sloth and her cub?

Still . . . kissing good night!